JOURNEY TO THE
CENTER OF THE EARTH

JULES VERNE

PLAYMORE PUBLISHERS

Editor: Heather Hammonds
Cover Illustration: Terry Riley
Illustrations: Terry Riley
Typesetting: Midland Typesetters

Journey to the Centre of the Earth
First published in 2008 by
Playmore Inc., Publishers,
58 Main Street, Hackensack, N.J. 07601

The Author
Jules Verne (1828–1905)

Jules Verne was one of the most popular writers of his time and has sometimes been called the father of science fiction.

Born in Nantes, France, Verne's father was a lawyer and his mother came from a family of ship builders, and seafarers. He was fascinated with travel from an early age and even tried to run away to sea when he was twelve. He studied law in Paris as a young man, but he soon gave up his studies to concentrate on his first love—writing.

The author of more than one hundred exciting novels, plays, and short stories, Verne accurately predicted many future scientific inventions and events, such as submarines, guided missiles, and space travel. He keenly studied the scientific discoveries of the time and wrote about them in many of his books.

Other successful novels by Verne include *From the Earth to the Moon, 20,000 Leagues Under the Sea* and *Around the World in 80 Days*, to name just a few.

Contents

Glossary

Words You Will Find in This Book:

chronometer an instrument measuring time very accurately

Cretaceous period a time in Earth's history between 144 million years ago and 65 million years ago

crustaceans shelled creatures such as crabs and shrimps

extinct died out—no more living examples of a plant or animal

fossils the remains of ancient animals or plants that have been preserved in rock

geology the study of the Earth and its rocks

ichthyosaur an extinct marine reptile that lived millions of years ago, during the Jurassic and Cretaceous periods

Jurassic period a time in Earth's history between 206 million years ago and 144 million years ago

lava	molten rock from a volcano
mastodon	a large elephant-like creature that became extinct around 10,000 years ago
plesiosaur	an extinct marine creature that lived millions of years ago, during the Jurassic and Cretaceous periods
runes	letters, or alphabets, of ancient languages
trilobite	an extinct hard-shelled marine creature that lived in Earth's seas around 300 million years ago
troglodyte	a cave dweller

Chapter 1
A Most Impatient Professor

The front door to our house flew open with a crash! My uncle, the distinguished scientist Professor Lidenbrock, hurried in. He flung his walking stick and broad-brimmed hat into a corner, and disappeared into his study.

I wasn't surprised at his dramatic appearance. He was an impatient man at the best of times and always in a hurry. Suddenly, I heard my name being called.

"Axel!" cried my uncle from his study. "Come here immediately!"

I had hardly moved one step forward when he called again. "Why haven't you got here yet?"

Yes, he was an impatient, selfish, and strange man at times. I often suspected his behavior might have been caused by studying such strange rocks as rhombohedrons, gehlenites, fangasites, and tungstates of manganese—not to mention writing a book called *Transcendental Crystallography*.

Professor Lidenbrock hurried in.

A Most Impatient Professor

The Professor, tall, thin, and about fifty years old, was a geologist; a man who studied the earth and its rocks. Indeed, his enthusiasm for his work had infected me with an interest and growing knowledge of the subject.

"Look what I have found!" he cried when I at last reached the study.

His eyes, which constantly rolled around behind huge spectacles, were circling more than usual; a very dangerous sign in the Professor.

"Isn't it beautiful?" he said, producing an ancient book I had seen him carry into the house.

"What is it?" I asked politely.

"This," explained the Professor, who could speak a dozen languages or more at the drop of a hat, "is an old manuscript written by Snorro Turleson, the famous Icelandic writer of the twelfth century. It's written in original Icelandic, an ancient language made up of letters called *runes*. It's said those runes were created by Odin himself. So they have sprung from the imagination of a god."

He then pulled out a piece of ancient parchment from the book. "And this," he continued, "is even more interesting."

I looked at the parchment. It was just a small scrap of paper that also contained some lines of runic letters. They were all gobbledygook and nonsense to me.

"I found this hidden inside the book," he said. "I recognize the runes but I have to admit, I haven't a clue what they mean."

Since runic letters always struck me as something invented by mad professors to mystify us ordinary mortals, it made me smile to see that my uncle was confused too.

A piece of ancient parchment.

At that moment Martha, the Professor's maid, put her head around the study door. "Supper's ready," she said. "The soup's on the table."

"Forget the soup," snapped my uncle, who had a habit of losing his temper when something was confusing him. "This is more important that guzzling soup!"

I was very hungry, so I left him to puzzle out the mystery by himself.

"I've never known Professor Lidenbrock not to come to supper," said Martha, shaking her head.

"That's worrying," I said.

"Yes, it is," she agreed solemnly. "It means something serious is going to happen. Mark my words."

I knew what she meant. There was no putting the Professor off the scent once he'd got a sniff of a mystery, scientific or otherwise. We were in for some extraordinary adventure. And that was scientific fact!

Chapter 2
The Code Unraveled

After supper, I returned to the study. My uncle was deep in thought, taking precise mathematical strides exactly three feet long, as he often did when he was trying to work out a problem.

"I have discovered something," he said. "The ancient book was written in the twelfth century by Turleson. But the parchment must have been written about two hundred years later. I believe that the person who owned the book must be the same person who wrote those runes on the parchment. And now I've found a name marked on the inside front cover of the book . . . Arne Saknussemm."

"And who is he?" I asked.

"Saknussemm was a famous sixteenth century Icelandic alchemist and traveler," replied my uncle. "He was renowned for his secrecy, so what we have on the parchment could be a secret code. It must contain something terribly important, otherwise he wouldn't have bothered to write it down in code. So we must crack this little mystery, mustn't we, my boy?"

"Yes Uncle," I answered, with little enthusiasm. I knew this could occupy us for weeks.

Over the next few days, the Professor tried everything to crack the code. First he translated the runic symbols into letters of the English alphabet. It simply produced three columns of nonsense.

He wasn't to be beaten. He played with the letters in every possible form. But the more ways he tried to solve the mystery, the more balderdash and twaddle he created.

He translated the letters into other languages, ancient Latin and Greek among them. Still he couldn't find an answer. But he thought the Latin translation looked hopeful. Next he read the letters from top to bottom, and upside-down. But still he found no answers.

My uncle crashed his fist on the table in frustration. "I know there is a message here somewhere, and I'm certain it is in Latin," he cried. "I can almost hear the author of this parchment trying to tell us his secret message!"

It was late that night when he finally decided to take some of the letters and lay

The Professor tried everything.

them out in a special order. He took the first letter of one line, followed by the first of the second. Then he repeated the operation on the third. He did this until he had a paragraph of unbroken letters.

The Professor stared at them and then banged his hand on the table again. "I thought I had it then," he said. "But this can't be it. Nothing makes sense."

He decided to go for a walk and think about the problem. When he had gone, I picked up the piece of paper on which he had written the letters. I read them.

mmessunkaSenrA.icefdoK.segnittamurtn ecertserrette,rotaivsadua,ednecsedsadne lacartniiiluJsiratracSarbmutabiledmek meretarcsilucoYsleffenSnI

I read the letters over and over. I tried to group them, to form words. It was impossible. My brain was becoming overheated with trying to read the code, so I picked up the piece of paper and started fanning myself with it. Then I began to laugh.

My uncle was right! By some fortunate accident, he had worked out the secret code. It was

I began to laugh.

in Latin. But he had tried to be too clever.

In fact, by fanning myself I started to see words as they flashed in front of my eyes. The letters didn't need deciphering. They only needed reading back to front.

When the Professor returned I showed him what I had found out.

Back to front, it read in Latin:

In Sneffels Yoculis craterem kem delibat
Umbra Scartaris Julii intra calendas descende,
Audas viator, et terrestre centrum attinges.
Kod feci, Arne Saknussemm

My uncle hastily translated the Latin into English.

Descend into the crater of Sneffels Yokul,
over which the shadow of Scartaris falls
before the kalends of July, bold traveler,
and you will reach the center of the Earth.
I have done this Arne Saknussemm.

On reading it my uncle gave a jump, as if he had been given an electric shock. He started walking up and down, holding his head in both hands. He moved the chairs and fiddled with piles of books.

At last, his nerves calmed down and he collapsed into an armchair.

"What time is it, Axel?" he asked.

"About three o'clock," I replied.

"Then hurry upstairs and pack your bags," he said.

Why should I want to pack? I wasn't going anywhere.

But then I began to think. If I understood this translation correctly, Saknussemm was claiming that he had descended into a crater and journeyed to the center of the Earth.

Surely it could not be true!

It was now clear to me why the Professor wanted me to pack. His next words didn't surprise me at all.

"We are about to embark on an extraordinary journey," he said. "Nothing less than an expedition to the center of the Earth!"

Chapter 3
Sheer Madness!

It was sheer madness to consider traveling to the center of the Earth! I knew that only a good scientific argument against the expedition would stop my uncle from setting off.

At supper that evening I tried to persuade him against the whole thing. But he wasn't listening to any scientific arguments, however strong. His mind was already halfway to the center of the Earth.

"Axel," he said, "you are a very clever young man, and you have done me a great service by solving the code. I shall never forget that, my boy, and you shall have your share in the glory we are going to win."

"Splendid," I thought. "We'll both be long dead before there is any glory to be had!"

"But above all," continued my uncle, "I must now insist on total secrecy. I have plenty of rivals in the world of science who would be only too keen to undertake this journey. They mustn't hear about this until we have returned."

"Do you really think that there are other scientists who would be bold enough to risk such a venture?" I asked.

"Of course, dear boy!" he roared. "Who would hesitate at the thought of winning such fame? If the discovery of the parchment was to be made public, a whole army of geologists would rush to follow in our footsteps."

"Are you sure that the document is genuine?" I asked.

"Of course it is," he replied.

"It might be a hoax," I pointed out.

"Stuff and nonsense," he said, twitching his shaggy eyebrows.

"What about the names then," I said. "*Yokul, Sneffels*, and *Scartaris*? Surely, they are not real places or people."

"They are places," he said calmly. "I'll show you."

Uncle went to his bookshelf and pulled out an atlas. He opened a page showing Iceland and pointed to the word *yokul*. The word could be seen in several places.

"It's an Icelandic word for volcanic mountains," he said.

Sheer Madness!

"I must now insist on total secrecy."

I hadn't given up yet. "And what about *Sneffels*?"

His finger searched for a moment and then came to rest on a remote corner of the country. "There is Sneffels," he answered. "It's an extinct volcano. And undoubtedly it will become the most famous volcano in the world, if its crater leads to the center of the Earth."

"Then what does *Scartaris* mean?" I asked. "And how do the *kalends of July* come into this?"

"Ah," he said, "I have only just worked that out. I've read somewhere that Sneffels has three chimneys; rocky funnels where the molten lava poured out when the volcano last erupted. Perhaps Saknussemm is giving us a clue to which one leads to the center of the Earth. Scartaris is a nearby volcano and the kalends of July simply means toward the end of July. My guess is that at that time the sun will cast the shadow of Scartaris on one of those chimneys. And whichever one it touches is the one Saknussemm took to begin his journey. Nothing could be more precise."

My uncle certainly had an answer to everything. I couldn't shake his belief that the parchment was genuine. So I took a different approach.

"There is Sneffels."

"Arne Saknussemm's directions are quite clear then," I said. "And the document does seem genuine. Perhaps he did go to Sneffels. Perhaps he did see the shadow of Scartaris. Perhaps he had even heard of legends about that crater leading to the center of the Earth. But what proof is there that he actually went there?"

My uncle returned my question with another. "And why couldn't he have gone to the center of the Earth?" he asked.

"Because," I said, "it is generally recognized that the temperature rises by about one degree for every seventy feet you go down. The Earth's radius—or for our purposes the exact distance to the center of the Earth—is four thousand miles or so. So the temperature at the center would be more than two million degrees."

"So it's the temperature that worries you," said Uncle.

"Of course," I said. "If we were to go down just twenty-five miles, the temperature would be more than 1,300 degrees."

"And you are afraid of melting away?" he asked, with a smile.

"A little," I sighed.

"Let me give you my views," he said. "Neither you nor anybody else knows for certain what is going on inside the Earth, seeing that mankind had only penetrated a few hundred feet into it so far. Answer me this. The number of active volcanoes is decreasing all the time. Doesn't that hint that perhaps the inside of the Earth is cooling?

"And what about the theory of tides inside the Earth? Perhaps there are cooling seas inside. I firmly believe that the internal heat of the Earth is nothing as hot as some scientists say. But the question doesn't matter for now. We shall get our answer when we get there."

It was useless. I now knew there was nothing I could say to change the Professor's mind.

Chapter 4
Our Journey Begins

I was very fond of my uncle, and he of me. But I still wasn't sure if I had been listening to the speculations of a mad professor or the scientific conclusions of a genius.

Later that day I went for a walk with Grauben. Grauben was my uncle's goddaughter and she lived with us, in his house. She was also my dearest friend.

As we walked, I told her of my uncle's plans. I thought she would be horrified, but she wasn't at all.

"What a wonderful thing it would be for a scientist and his nephew to make such a journey," she said. "You'll both become famous. I would do anything to come with you."

I was too ashamed to admit to a young woman who I loved and admired that the idea terrified me. "You'll think differently when it comes to it," I said.

Walking with Grauben.

"Never!" she replied, "I would love to go."

"In any case," I thought, "the kalends of July are still a long way off. There's still time to persuade my uncle not to go."

How wrong I was. When we reached the house, I found the Professor unloading a cart full of things he had bought that afternoon; rope ladders, torches, grappling irons, pick-axes, tough walking boots, flasks to hold water, backpacks, gunpowder, and guns.

Why had he bought two Colt revolvers and two rifles? Surely there were no wild beasts or savages living at the center of the Earth.

He had also bought a thermometer, an instrument to measure air pressure, a chronometer to tell the time and keep a record of the days, a compass to check our directions, and three brand new portable electric lamps.

In addition, he had bought a lot of food; mainly long-lasting meat extract. I'd already heard the Professor say he wouldn't be taking great stocks of water. "We'll find plenty underground," he'd said.

"Come on, Axel," he cried on seeing me. "Hurry up! Your box isn't even packed yet."

I was thunderstruck. My voice almost failed me. "Are we going?" I said at last.

"Of course," he replied. "We leave at dawn, the day after tomorrow."

Inside the house, I found the hallway piled with more equipment that my uncle had bought.

I hardly slept at all that night, I was so worried. The next day I asked Uncle why we had to leave so soon. "It's only the beginning of May," I said.

"You silly boy," he said impatiently. "Do you think it's that easy to get to Iceland? Only one ship a month sails there. And if we don't take this month's ship, we'll arrive too late to see the shadow of Scartaris touch the correct chimney in the crater of Sneffels. Now will you *please* go and pack your things."

Martha helped me pack. She asked me where we were going. I pointed toward the center of the Earth. "Into the cellar?" asked the old lady.

"No," I replied with a little tremble. "A bit farther down than that."

Martha simply shrugged her shoulders and sighed.

That night was worse than the one before. I dreamed about falling down a bottomless abyss and sinking into boiling quicksand. I

Martha asked me where we were going.

awoke at dawn, worn out from the terrible nightmare. I went downstairs to find my uncle eating a hearty breakfast. I couldn't eat a thing.

At half-past eight, a large carriage arrived to take us—and all the equipment—to the railway station.

Grauben kissed me goodbye and we promised each other that we would marry on my return. Not that I imagined I would ever be her husband. If there was one thing I was sure of at that moment, it was that I would never survive the journey!

We boarded the train and my fate was sealed. There was no turning back now.

As we left Hamburg behind us, the Professor didn't talk at all. His thoughts were obviously far ahead of the train. Later, he started examining the small case where he kept all his private possessions. I saw that he had the parchment safely tucked into his wallet.

The train took us to Kiel, from where we embarked on a boat for Denmark. Another train finally took us to Copenhagen, the Danish capital. We stayed there for two days before boarding a ship for Iceland. She was called the *Valkyrie.*

The name of that ship didn't give me much

cheer. *Valkyrie* was an ancient Scandinavian word for handmaidens who waited by the battlefield to carry off the dead!

Chapter 5
Iceland

The *Valkyrie* took ten days to reach Reykjavik, the capital city of Iceland. As we sailed toward the shore, my uncle took me aside and pointed across the water to a high mountain with two peaks, standing on a peninsula.

"Sneffels," he said quietly. "Sneffels. But keep silent, my boy. We must keep secrecy at all times."

That evening we stayed in Reykjavik. "Well," said the Professor, "I think the worst is over."

"The worst?" I asked in a puzzled voice.

"Yes, of course," he said. "The dreadful sea journey is over. I always feel so seasick. But I've recovered. Now we have nothing to do but go down."

"If that's how you look at it, Uncle," I said, "you may be right. But don't forget that when we have gone down, we'll have to come up again."

Pointing to a high mountain.

"Oh, that doesn't worry me," he said. "By then we'll be famous, whether we're alive or dead!"

We were invited to stay at the home of Mr. Fridriksson, a distinguished science master in the city's main school. My uncle made a point of not telling him anything about our mission, except to say that we wanted to explore the Sneffels region.

Mr. Fridriksson introduced us to a hunter called Hans Bjelke, who said he would happily come with us as a guide. Hans was a large man with long red hair and an intelligent face. He looked like a very calm character, a good man in a crisis.

My uncle took one look at Hans and instantly recognized him as a man of rare qualities. "I think we could do with a fellow like that on our great journey," he whispered to me.

We discovered that Hans was a man of few words. In fact, if he said two words in a day that was a lot for him. He only used one word when my uncle asked him if he would like to go on an extraordinary journey with us.

"Yes," he replied, without even questioning where or why we were going.

At dawn on 15 June, we loaded all our equipment onto two pack horses.

With everyone still asleep in Reykjavik, we quietly left the city. We were on our way to the center of the Earth!

I began to feel a little happier as we rode quietly away from Reykjavik. The sun was rising on a beautiful day. I felt like a carefree tourist in a new land.

"Besides," I said to myself, "where's the risk if we climb a tall mountain? Where's the risk in, at worst, walking down into the crater of an extinct volcano? As for the existence of a passage leading to the center of the Earth —that has to be pure imagination and an absolute impossibility."

We followed a route along the winding coastline. We traveled for the whole day, finally stopping for the night in a small settlement. Of course, there was no real night. It was midsummer and we were so close to the North Pole that the sun did not set at this time of the year.

We continued on the next day. As we drew closer to Sneffels, I began to lose my carefree attitude. "How does anyone know if Sneffels is an extinct volcano?" I thought, as we set off again the next day. "What will happen if the

On our way to the center of the Earth!

volcano suddenly becomes active again while we are inside the crater?"

I went to see my uncle and explained my fears.

He tried to calm me. "I have been thinking about the same thing," he said. "Sneffels may well roar again, but not this week. New eruptions are always preceded by certain signals. The people in Reykjavik assured me that Sneffels is deeply asleep for now."

His words calmed me a little, although the steady stream of steam coming from the summit of the monster still made me nervous.

Now we were into the foothills of the volcano. For the next few hours, we battled our way up the steep slopes. It was bitterly cold and the wind was blowing hard. My legs were starting to fail me, as we climbed the final 1,500 feet through bleak streams of cold, solid lava.

After five hours of climbing, we reached the summit. I was shattered, gasping for breath in the thin mountain air on top of the crater ring of Sneffels.

"Now somewhere down there," said my uncle, pointing to the bottom of the crater, "we will begin our descent into the center of the Earth!"

Chapter 6
Descent into the Crater

The next day we left the pack horses behind and loaded our equipment and provisions into our backpacks. Then the Professor led us down into the crater. It was so steep that we had to fasten ourselves together by rope, to keep from falling.

By noon we had arrived at the bottom. It was an awe-inspiring sight to look up to where we had come from. We were dwarfed by the sharply rising sides of the crater walls looming above us.

At the bottom of the crater we found the three massive rock chimneys. The Professor was like an excited child, rushing about everywhere, examining them from every angle. Suddenly, he gave a shout.

"Axel! Hans! Come here!" he cried.

Hans and I went over to him.

"Look!" he said, pointing at a rock, at the base of the chimneys.

"Axel! Hans! Come here!"

I saw some familiar runic characters engraved on its rough surface.

They said one thing: *Arne Saknussemm.*

"Have you any doubts now?" asked my uncle, still staring at the spot where Saknussemm had left his mark.

I shook my head, rather overwhelmed by the evidence of the runic characters engraved on the stone.

That night Hans and I slept on a bed of lava rock. But my uncle refused to go to sleep. He spent the whole night pacing around the crater like a wild beast caught in a deep pit. He couldn't wait to continue our adventure.

I slept a little, but I couldn't help imagining that I heard tremors echoing around the sides of the crater. I desperately hoped that an eruption was not on its way.

The next day a gray, heavy sky settled over the volcano summit above us. It put my uncle in a very bad mood.

He knew that, according to the words on the parchment, Arne Saknussemm had climbed down one of the three chimneys and that the shadow of Scartaris would touch the edge of the correct chimney during the last days of June.

It was now 25 June, and if the clouds hid the sun for much longer there would be no shadow to show us the correct one. The expedition would have to be canceled for another year.

The day wore on and no shadow appeared on the bottom of the crater. My uncle did not speak to me all day. He gazed up at the leaden skies, praying for the sun to break through.

On 26 June, there was still no sign of the sun. The Professor was beside himself with frustration.

He gazed up at the leaden skies.

It rained all day on 27 June. Hans, who had been sleeping for most of the last three days, beckoned to my uncle. "A change in the weather will be here by tomorrow," he said. "I can feel it coming."

This was the longest sentence Hans had spoken since he'd joined us.

That evening my uncle revealed to Hans the true nature of our mission. One would have thought that anyone would have run a mile on being asked to make a journey to the center of the Earth. But not Hans. He hardly blinked an eyelid.

"Where you go," he said, "I will follow."

The next day, 28 June, dawned bright and sunny. The sun poured its rays into the crater, casting a shadow on every hillock, rock, and stone. As it moved across the sky, it brought the shadow of Scartaris ever closer to us. At exactly midday, the moving shadow finally came to rest on the central chimney.

"The sun has shown us the way to go!" cried my uncle, happy at last. "We must travel down the central chimney!"

We put on our heavy backpacks and approached the central chimney. Being an impatient man, my uncle had a quick solution for all the unbreakable items we needed, such as a change of clothes. He simply threw them into the chimney. We would, hopefully, find them again as we climbed down.

I had not even dared to look down the chimney yet. But Hans seemed to be treating the expedition as a Sunday outing. That gave me some encouragement, so I clambered up the side.

At the top, I leaned over an overhanging rock and looked down. The chimney was about a hundred feet across. My legs started to shake and my hair stood on end. I had never feared heights or depths before, but looking down the chimney made me feel quite giddy with fear.

The inside of the chimney had steep vertical walls disappearing into the abyss. Those walls were covered in cracks and rocky outcrops which made climbing look reasonably easy.

But if the "staircase" was there, the "banisters" were missing. There was nothing much to hold onto as we descended. So my uncle uncoiled one of our longest rope ladders and let it drop into the abyss. He secured one end to an overhanging rock with a special knot that could be untied with a quick jerk from below, when—or if—we got down there.

Throwing our belongings into the chimney.

"Right!" he said. "I think it is time to begin our descent."

My legs began to shake with fear . . .

Chapter 7
Into the Unknown

None of us said a word as we began our climb down the volcanic chimney. Hans led the party, followed by my uncle, and then me. It was a question of slowly climbing down the gently swaying ladder, stopping now and again to rest our legs on some rocky lava outcrop.

I wondered if the ladder would actually hold three people. I expected it to break at any moment and send us tumbling to our deaths.

Hans was wonderful. As soon as we got going, he encouraged my uncle and me all the way. "Be careful," he kept saying. "We are doing well so far."

Every now and then our feet dislodged small pieces of rock. It seemed ages before we heard them hit something, far below us.

After half an hour we landed on a flat surface inside the chimney. My uncle tugged at the rope and freed it from its anchor at the top.

On the way down I had been too frightened to even think of studying the geology of the rocks that we passed. I wouldn't have known if we had passed through the age of the Cretaceous or Jurassic!

But the Professor had been examining everything. "The farther I go," he said, "the more confident I feel in understanding the earth's crust."

He then repositioned the rope and we continued on down. After three hours I still could not see the bottom of the chimney. But when I raised my head, I saw the opening way above us, getting smaller and smaller. The walls were closing in on us. It was gradually getting darker.

Still we kept descending, resetting the rope ladder every now and again to continue on down. Now, when we dislodged rocks and stones, we could hear them landing a lot sooner than before. We were getting close to the bottom of the abyss.

I was now a little more relaxed, and began to keep count of the number of times we dropped the rope to descend on the next stage. I knew that the rope was some 30 feet long and each climb took about thirty minutes.

Climbing down the ladder.

So I could calculate precisely what depth we had reached, and roughly how much time had passed. We had now changed the rope fourteen times, so I estimated that we had descended nearly three thousand feet already.

Once more we landed on a flat surface. "We've reached the bottom of the chimney," announced the Professor, as calmly as if we had reached a railway destination.

We were in an enormous rock cavern. At either end of the cavern was a tunnel. One tunnel went in an easterly direction, the other west. The bags of unbreakable items that my uncle had thrown down the chimney were lying nearby. The long journey down hadn't damaged anything.

"We'll see about those tunnels tomorrow," said my uncle, as we picked up the bags. "Let's have some supper and then get some sleep."

We opened our bag of provisions and ate a meal, before settling down as best we could to sleep on a bed of stones and bits of lava. Lying on my back, I found myself looking up the three thousand foot chimney. It was like a giant telescope.

The entrance to the chimney so far above

We were in an enormous rock cavern.

us, now seemed tiny. Yet, I managed to catch sight of the bright evening star, just before falling into an exhausted sleep.

I awoke several hours later, to find that my uncle was already up.

"Well, Axel," he said. "Have you ever spent such a restful night? If we had been at home there would be carts rumbling past the window and market fellows making a great din. It's peaceful down here, don't you think?"

"It may be very quiet," I replied, "but the quieter it gets, the scarier it seems."

"Come, come," he said. "If you're frightened already, what will you be like later on? So far we've hardly touched the Earth's surface."

"What do you mean?" I asked.

"I mean, we have only descended to sea level," he said.

"What will happen when we go deeper and the air pressure builds up?" I asked. "Will breathing be difficult?"

"No," he replied. "We shall descend slowly and our lungs will get used to breathing a denser atmosphere. Aeronauts suffer from a lack of air when they rise into the sky. We will suffer from the opposite. But we'll get used to it."

We had a small breakfast of biscuits and water before preparing to leave our first camp.

"Now," said the Professor, in an excited voice, "we are really going to plunge into the depths of the Earth!"

Chapter 8
Ten Thousand Feet Below Sea Level

The Professor took an immediate decision to investigate the eastern tunnel. It looked very dark and uninviting but he got out his electrical lamps and managed to successfully get all three going. "Right!" he said. "Let's go."

I took one last look upward at the dot of light far above me. I thought it might be the last time I ever saw daylight. My uncle's next comment didn't cheer me much, either.

"The records show," he said, "that the last time this volcano erupted was in the year 1229. If we had been here then, we would have been melted into nothing as the lava forced its way along this passage, on its way to the top."

Whenever he said things like that my imagination always began to work too hard. I thought I could hear rumblings again, coming from below.

Investigating the eastern tunnel.

Despite my misgivings, we made good progress. Our only problem was that the tunnel sloped downward at a very steep angle. We were in danger of slipping all the way down.

Even I was starting to enjoy the beauty of the place. "It's magnificent!" I exclaimed. "What a sight! Look at all the different shades of lava. And those crystals look like lighted globes."

"So you're beginning to appreciate it, are you Axel?" smiled the Professor. "If you think this is exciting, wait until we get even deeper. Now, quick march!"

The deeper we went, the more I was surprised that the temperature hardly rose at all. Perhaps my uncle had been right. Perhaps we weren't going to be melted alive. I looked at the thermometer we had with us and saw that the temperature had only risen a couple of degrees.

Without the use of the rope ladder, I could no longer work out how deep we had gone. But my uncle was measuring the depth by regularly measuring the angles of our slope downward and the distance traveled.

"My calculations now put us at ten thousand feet below sea level," he announced late that afternoon.

I was astounded. We had made such quick progress.

About eight o'clock in the evening, he called a halt. We had supper and drank a few sips from the water flasks we had brought with us. My uncle was certain that we would find plenty of underground water supplies, but I hadn't seen a drop anywhere so far.

"Don't worry," he said. "I assure you that we'll soon find all the water we could possibly need."

Eating our supper.

51

The next day, 30 June, we began another descent along the next stage of the lava-lined tunnel. Now we were passing beneath great arches of rock, as if we were in some enormous cathedral. It was quite an easy day's walking. But we were fast asleep as soon as we had wrapped ourselves in our traveling rugs that night.

It was quite strange how relaxed we had become. Even I began to question why I had been frightened. Why, there were no giants or other monstrous creatures down here! There was nothing to fear except an eruption, which was highly unlikely.

We resumed our journey the next day in good spirits. But soon after leaving our camp we found ourselves climbing, rather than descending.

"If this goes on much longer," grumbled my uncle, "we'll resurface in Iceland by tomorrow."

Chapter 9
Primitive Life

The tunnel continued upward and our back-packs seemed to be getting heavier all the time. My uncle was leading now, with Hans behind him. My main thought was to make sure I kept up with them. I shuddered at the idea of finding myself lost in this underground maze.

Soon, there was a change in the type of rocks making up the walls of the tunnel. Where lava had coated the rocks, making them rough, they were now smooth and solid.

My knowledge of geology was not as good as my uncle's. But I knew all the periods of geological history. I made a guess that we had reached rocks that were formed at the period when the first plants and animals appeared on Earth.

I was right. My feet had grown accustomed to the hard rocky tunnel. But now we were walking on a mix of dust and debris which had come from plant material and shells. On the walls were distinct impressions of primitive

weeds and mosses. There were fossils everywhere.

I found a perfectly preserved shell which
had belonged to an animal rather similar to the
modern-day wood louse. I hurried forward and
caught up with my uncle. "Look at this!" I said.

"Well," he said, "it's the shell of a trilobite.
Trilobites are an extinct species of crustacean."

I was amazed.

My uncle was not his normal positive self
that day. He was worried about our route. "I
think I may have made a mistake," he said.
"We're climbing too much. Perhaps we should
have taken the other tunnel."

I too was becoming worried. "We are getting
very short of water," I said.

"In that case, Axel," replied the Professor,
"we must ration ourselves until we find some
more."

It wasn't a very helpful answer because the
amount of water left in our flasks was unlikely
to last more than three days, even if we did
ration it.

By the end of the day we had entered a high
rocky gallery. We were passing beneath a series
of huge arches, the supporting rocks gleaming
in the light of the electric lamps.

There were fossils everywhere.

Most of the rocks seemed to contain remains of life. As well as the very primitive sea creatures such as trilobites, there were remains of early fish and lizards. We were among rocks that had been formed on the bed of an ancient sea. Time had stood still down here, beneath the surface of the Earth.

We were all starting to feel very thirsty as we set off again the next day.

Around the middle of the day I saw that the rocks were changing yet again. The lamps were now shining on a dark substance. I put out a hand to touch the wall and when I took it away, it was covered in black dust. I suddenly realized we were in a coalfield!

In the evening, the three of us sat beneath the walls of coal and drank the few drops of water that we rationed ourselves. Then Hans prepared some food. Soon we were all asleep, exhausted after our journey.

The next day was Saturday—although the days had very little meaning so deep underground. We set off again and soon entered a vast cavern. It was at least 100 feet wide and 150 feet high. The floor had been torn apart by some volcanic disturbance.

I was acutely aware that, apart from Arne

Saknussemm—if indeed he had come this way—we were the first human beings to see this sight.

Despite my uncle's theories that the interior depths of the Earth had cooled, we saw our first fires here. A particularly violent blaze was happening high up in the cavern, although we could not see what was causing it.

The air was heavy with gases. I've no doubt that my uncle's decision to bring his electric lighting devices saved our lives here. A naked flame could well have set off a devastating explosion.

The electric lamps were not very powerful. It was always dark around twenty yards ahead of us. So it came as a nasty surprise when we suddenly found ourselves up against a wall of rock. There was no way through. We had come to a dead end.

"Well, so much the better," said my uncle. "At least we know where we stand now. There's nothing to do but turn back."

It was agreed that we would get some sleep before leaving.

"All is not lost," he continued. "We'll be back to the gallery beneath the crater within three days."

We saw our first fires.

"If we have the strength," I replied.

"And why shouldn't we, Axel?"

"Because tomorrow we shall have no water left," I replied gloomily.

Chapter 10

Christopher Columbus of the Underworld

The next day we set off early. As I had foreseen, the water gave out after a few hours. It wasn't long before we were suffering from severe thirst.

By the second day, we were running out of energy.

On the third day, we all found it difficult to keep walking. I kept passing out. Hans and my uncle encouraged me on, despite their own suffering.

At last, crawling on our hands and knees, we reached the junction of the two tunnels beneath the crater. I immediately collapsed into a deep sleep. When I awoke, I found myself in my uncle's arms. He was pouring a little water from his flask down my throat.

Oh what bliss I knew at that moment! Just a mouthful of water slaked my burning thirst. I thanked my uncle with clasped hands.

I found myself in my uncle's arms.

"It was the very last of the water," he said. "I saved it for emergencies. There is definitely no more now."

Up until then, I had thought my uncle had been rather grumpy and bad-tempered. But now I saw what a kind man he truly was. He had given me his last drop of water.

That tiny drop of water gave me some new strength. I even managed to speak again. "We must return to the surface while we still can," I said. "We can't go on without water."

"Go back?" my uncle gasped.

"Yes, we must," I nodded.

"I kept that last drop of water for you," he said, "but it doesn't seem to have restored your courage."

"What!" I cried. "You don't want to go back?"

"And give up this expedition, just when success seems assured?" he said. "Never!"

"Then we must resign ourselves to dying," I sighed.

"I have begun this journey and I mean to either finish it or never return," he said firmly.

My uncle tried to calm my worries about water. "Listen to me," he said, "once we get a little way down the right tunnel, we'll reach levels formed by granite. And there's bound to be water there."

"But what if there isn't?" I asked.

"Remember Christopher Columbus," he said. "His crew was so sick they asked to go home. He begged them to give him three more days. He promised them that if he hadn't found anything by then, he would turn back. The next day he discovered America. Axel, all I ask of you is one more day. Think of me as the Christopher Columbus of the underworld. If after a day we have found no water, I swear to you that we will return to the surface."

"All I ask of you is one more day."

I was touched by his words. If he was prepared to give up his dream if we didn't find water within a day, then I was willing to battle on for another twenty-four hours.

"Well," I said, "I agree. And may the ancient Icelandic gods reward your superhuman energy. Let's be on our way."

So the descent began again, this time by the western tunnel. We had only gone a few hundred yards down it when the Professor called out, "These are very primitive rocks we've reached. We are definitely on the right track now."

Once more we found ourselves marching down a tunnel that had once been a volcanic vent, a major artery through which the molten rock of ancient times had passed on its way to the surface.

This tunnel was full of twists and turns, with numerous galleries leading off it.

Down, down, down we went, regularly passing changes in rock structure. The farther down we went, the closer we came to the granite levels.

On the way down we saw outcrops of copper with occasional traces of platinum and gold that glistened under Uncle's electrical lamps. Despite my dreadful thirst, I was fascinated to see these fabulous riches so well

I was fascinated by the fabulous riches.

hidden from the greedy eyes of mankind.

These treasures had been buried so deep by the convulsions of the Earth's early days, that neither pickaxe nor mining drill would ever be able to extract them from their hiding place.

Deeper still, and we finally reached the first layers of granite. But there was still no sign of water. I was suffering agonies of thirst, as were Hans and my uncle. We carried on, traveling in the hope of hearing the sound of a rushing spring. But there was no welcome sound of water.

Finally, my legs began to fail me. I bore my torments as well as I could, if only because that single day belonged to my uncle. But at last my strength gave out completely. I gave a cry and collapsed to the ground.

My uncle turned back, gazing at me as I lay on the ground. "It's all over," he said. "It's the end."

I passed out. When I opened my eyes again, I saw my two companions lying in their sleeping rugs. Were they asleep? I couldn't tell. My uncle's last words—*It's all over*—echoed in my ears. I knew that in my present state of weakness, I had no hope of returning to the surface. I also knew my uncle would never leave me.

Christopher Columbus of the Underworld

We now had more than four miles of the Earth's crust above us. And that great mass seemed to be bearing down with all its weight on my shoulders. I hadn't even the strength to turn over on my hard granite bed.

Chapter 11
Water!

It was very quiet, so deep underground. I was sure no sound could reach us through the walls of rock that surrounded us like a granite coffin. Yet, in the midst of my drowsiness, I thought I heard something deep within that rock.

Just then, I saw Hans get up. He picked up an electric lamp and walked off silently down the tunnel, the light from his lamp disappearing as he turned a corner. A few moments later the sound of Hans's footsteps died away to nothing. Uncle and I were left alone with the dim light of the one remaining lamp.

At first I thought Hans was abandoning us. Then I realized that the route he had taken would lead him farther down into the Earth. If he'd meant to leave us, he would have taken the upward path. Besides, he had proved a good and loyal servant so far. Those thoughts calmed my worries a little. Perhaps he had

I thought Hans was abandoning us.

heard the same faint sounds I had heard, and had gone to investigate.

For a whole hour, I dreamed up ideas of what Hans might be doing. Then at last I heard the sound of footsteps returning. He was coming up again. A few moments later the shadow of Hans appeared, as he came around the final corner.

Hans went up to my uncle, put his hand on his shoulder, and gently woke him.

My uncle stirred. "What is it, Hans?"

Hans pointed down the tunnel and uttered just one word: "Water."

Despite our exhausted states, my uncle and I were on our feet in moments, and were soon hurrying forward. It was downhill all the way. Suddenly Hans stopped and indicated with his finger for us to keep quiet. The sound was quite clear now.

"Clever Hans," said my uncle. "That's the sound of a subterranean stream. It's very close."

We hurried on. I was no longer tired. Just the sound of running water had refreshed me.

Finally, Hans stopped and took a pickaxe from his pack. He went to the wall of the tunnel, put his ear to it and listened for a moment. Then he nodded, and began to dig at the rock with his pickaxe.

How he kept going, I'll never know. But for two hours he worked on that rock, chipping away at it bit by bit. I was beginning to lose hope again when suddenly, there was a hissing sound. He had broken through!

At first it was just a trickle, but soon there was a good steady flow of water pouring from the hole. I leapt across, and using my hands as a cup, reached out for a drink. I plunged my hands into the stream. "Ouch!" I screamed.

The water was almost boiling.

"Don't worry," said my uncle, "it'll cool down."

The tunnel filled with steam as a stream of hot water flowed swiftly down the passage. We filled our flasks and waited for the water to cool. At last we could drink and relieve our thirst.

The water must have come from a major underground source, for the stream didn't slow or dry up at all. We were thinking of blocking up the hole Hans had made in case we flooded ourselves out. But the water flowed at a steady rate, and didn't seem to be filling the tunnel.

In the end, we decided to leave it open

Hans had broken through!

because we saw that we had now created a permanent stream, right beside our downward path. The stream would always move downhill, so we would not be short of water again.

We were so grateful to Hans for finding the water that we named the stream after him. He smiled in gratitude but then settled back to his usual quiet ways.

What joy that water gave us, even when it was still warm. But when it cooled it was exquisitely refreshing after all our suffering. It brought us all back to life.

After a while I noticed its taste. "There's a lot of iron in it," I said to Uncle.

"Of course," he replied. "And it's good for you. People would pay us a lot of money if we could bottle this sort of spring water."

Chapter 12
Deeper, Ever Deeper

The next morning we had breakfast, and plenty of water to refresh us for the journey ahead. I was in much better spirits. I even started to think that with a man as determined as Uncle and another as useful as Hans, there was every chance we might make it to the center of the Earth.

If anyone had suggested now that we return to the crater, I would have refused with great indignation. All we had to do was descend another few thousand miles, and we would be there.

We set off down the granite tunnel again. It twisted and turned, and opened up into more huge rocky galleries. My uncle kept consulting his compass to check our direction.

The stream we had created was running beside us still. It was like a refreshing spirit, guiding us on our way. We were making very good progress. That evening the Professor

The stream was running beside us.

estimated that we were seventy-five miles south-west of Reykjavik and seven miles down.

We were about to set up camp for the night when we came upon what my uncle was sure was a fault; a split in the granite mass. It had obviously been formed by the cooling of the Earth's crust.

I looked down the crack. It was just wide enough to climb down, but the darkness below was not a welcoming sight.

The darkness didn't worry the Professor. He took one look down and clapped his hands in excitement. "Now we'll make good progress, without much effort," he said. "The crack will make a perfect staircase."

I had some serious doubts about that.

We linked ourselves together by ropes and began the descent. We were soon soaking wet because our stream was still following us. We weren't cold, though, as there was still a pleasant heat coming from the water.

Every fifteen minutes we would stop to rest, and relieve our aching leg muscles. We would sit down on some projecting rock, with our legs dangling in space as we ate some of our food.

Eating some of our food.

We followed the fault for the next two days, penetrating another five miles into the Earth's crust. By 15 July we were eighteen miles down. Although we were a little tired, we were feeling fit and healthy.

My uncle did his daily reading of his compass, chronometer, and thermometer. When he told me that we were now 125 miles from Sneffels, I could hardly believe him.

"Why are you so surprised?" he asked.

"Well, Uncle," I answered, "I think that means we are no longer beneath Iceland."

"Indeed not," he said. "We are now under the sea."

The Professor wasn't concerned about our location at all. But I was a little uneasy at the thought of that mass of water over my head. I just hoped that an earthquake wouldn't split the granite and send the sea down onto us!

Over the next few days, the fault widened into a steep tunnel that quickly took us to very great depths.

On Saturday, 18 July, the tunnel opened up into an enormous grotto. We decided to camp there for the night. The grotto formed a huge hall, with our faithful stream flowing over its floor.

As I lay in my sleeping rug after dinner, I thought about how well accustomed the three of us had become to our troglodyte existence. I hardly gave a thought now to the sun, stars, and the moon; nor trees, houses, and towns. Our needs miles beneath other humans were more modest. We needed very little in the way of human comforts.

After breakfast the next morning, the Professor announced he was going to spend a few hours getting his scientific notes in order. "I am going to work out our exact position," he said. "When we get back I want to be able to draw a map of our journey; a sort of vertical map which will show the course of our expedition. I don't want to make any mistakes."

Uncle took a whole series of new readings from his instruments and announced that we had now come 213 miles from our starting point.

"So we are indeed traveling under the Atlantic," I said.

"Exactly," he nodded.

"And what depth are we at today?" I asked.

"Forty-eight miles," he replied.

"But isn't that the limit of the thickness of

the Earth's crust?" I asked anxiously.

"Yes, if you believe latest scientific theory," he said.

"And here, by that same theory," I said, "it should be 1,500 degrees centigrade. We should be in boiling hot molten lava by now."

"Yes, we should be," he replied, "if you believe the latest talk of the scientists. But you can see for yourself that firstly, we are still in solid rock and secondly, it's just pleasantly warm. It's precisely twenty-seven degrees cen-

The professor worked on his notes.

tigrade. As so often happens, those armchair scientists befuddle us with their guesses and strange ideas."

"Well the scientists are only 1,473 degrees out," I laughed.

Chapter 13
Lost and Alone

It must be admitted that so far things had gone fairly well. I had little cause to complain. We were all still alive, after all. And that surprised me enormously!

But the Professor's current findings gave me a new concern. "If the Earth's radius is about four thousand miles and we have only descended forty-eight miles in twenty days," I said to him, "then by my calculations, if we continue at the same rate, it will take us five and a half years to reach the center."

"To blazes with your calculations, my boy," he replied gruffly. "What are they based on? How do you know that this passage doesn't lead straight down to our destination? Remember, we have evidence that another man has already reached the center—one Arne Saknussemm. Where he succeeded, I shall succeed too."

I wasn't convinced. And what if Saknussemm *had* reached the center of the Earth?

How did he know he had actually arrived there? After all, in the sixteenth century, he didn't have the advanced navigation equipment that my uncle had.

Of course, I didn't dare say that to my uncle.

For the next few days the tunnel led us down some very severe inclines, and through some enormous galleries. This was a dangerous descent and Hans's skill with the climbing ropes was called for. That calm and helpful Icelander got us out of a lot of scrapes on those steep slopes.

For most of that period of time, the journey was quite boring and uneventful. By 7 August we had reached a depth of seventy miles, and were five hundred miles from Iceland.

It was a day I shall never forget. We were going down a very gentle slope. I was walking alone. My uncle and Hans were some way behind me. I was carrying one of the electric lamps and I remember stopping to examine some rocks.

A few minutes later, I looked back and was astonished to discover that I was alone! Where had the Professor and Hans gone? They had been behind me. Had they overtaken me? I was sure they hadn't. They couldn't possibly

A dangerous descent.

have passed me without my seeing them. For a few moments I wondered what to do.

I decided that the only thing to do was to retrace my footsteps by going back.

For the next fifteen minutes, I hurried back the way I thought I had come, looking around for any signs of my fellow travelers. I found and heard nobody. I called out but got no reply. My voice lost itself in a cavernous gallery.

I began to feel very uneasy and a shiver ran down my spine. "I must keep calm," I said to myself. "I'm sure to find Uncle and Hans soon. There's only one path, after all. As I was in front, they must be somewhere behind me."

For the next half hour I continued walking, stopping every few yards to listen for anyone calling me. But an extraordinary silence filled the underground world. I could not believe I was alone. I might have gone a little astray, but I could not be lost.

"Come on!" I said to myself. "I'm sure to find them. Where could they have gone? All I have to do is to keep on going and we'll bump into each other."

But, deep down, I was beginning to doubt whether I would ever see them again. In fact, in my growing panic, I had begun to doubt every-

"Where could they have gone?"

thing. Had I really been in front? Perhaps I had really been behind them. But if I hadn't seen them pass me, surely I must have been ahead. I was so confused.

Suddenly, I remembered the stream. "How can I get lost when I have an unbreakable thread to guide me?" I whispered. "I will always have the faithful stream with me. I have only to follow it backward and I am sure to find my companions."

This conclusion lifted my spirits. Before I set off again, I decided to refresh myself in the stream. I bent down to plunge my head into the water. To my horror, I found myself standing on rough, dry granite. The stream was no longer flowing at my feet!

Chapter 14
Darkness and Despair

To describe my despair at that moment would be impossible. I was buried alive deep beneath the Atlantic Ocean, with the prospect of dying from the tortures of hunger and thirst.

But how had I come to lose my companions and the life-giving stream? One moment they were there, the next they had gone. There was only one explanation. There must have been a fork in the passage somewhere. Maybe my companions—and the stream—had taken a different path.

That was the only conclusion I could come to. My uncle and Hans must have gone down the passage with the stream, while I had taken another. Now I was truly lost and alone, with seventy-five miles of rock above me. I felt crushed already.

I tried to turn my thoughts to more familiar things; the city of Hamburg, my home, my street, and my poor Grauben. But it didn't

Now I was truly lost and alone.

help. Instead I thought that I must be mad if I had any hopes of returning to my home and my loved ones.

"Oh, Uncle!" I exclaimed in a desperate voice.

I knew that he must be suffering as much as me. He and Hans must be out there somewhere, searching for me.

My water flask was full and I had enough food for at least another three days. After that, I was finished. I decided to continue walking back, hoping to find the stream again. If I found the stream, then I could at least follow it to the hole that Hans had broken in the wall. From there, I might just be able to find my way to the chimney vent that led to the surface.

I set off again, passing through the galleries and passages. I walked along, hoping and praying I would be found. I examined every corner and rocky outcrop, but I saw no familiar landmarks. And rather than find the place where we had discovered the water, I hit a dead end.

A massive granite boulder blocked my way. There was no way around it. My sense of loneliness and terror increased tenfold. I was sure now that there was no hope of my finding a

A massive granite boulder blocked my way.

way out. I was doomed to die the most horrible of deaths.

An awful thought crossed my mind, at that point. I was traveling in a world of fossils. What would future scientists think in millions of years' time, if they found my fossilized body seventy-five miles beneath the Earth's surface?

In the midst of all my anxiety, a new terror took hold of me. I had damaged my electric lamp. I had no means of repairing it and it was failing. I watched the glow from the electrical current gradually fading, creating a strange procession of moving shadows along the darkening walls.

Finally, a last gleam flickered in the lamp. I watched it anxiously, concentrating the full power of my eyes on it. I was sure it was the last light I would ever see.

Then it went out. I was plunged into unfathomable darkness.

A terrible cry burst from my lips. On Earth, even on the darkest night, light never entirely vanishes. Here there was none. The total darkness made me a blind man.

At this point I lost my head. I stood up with my arms stretched out before me, trying to feel my way. Then, in panic, I started running haphazardly through the rocky maze, always expecting to dash my head to pieces on sharp rocks. I cried and yelled at the top of my voice. There was no friendly reply.

Utterly exhausted, I eventually fainted and fell headlong to the floor.

Chapter 15
The Echo of Voices

When I regained consciousness, my face was wet with tears. I cannot say how long I had been unconscious because I no longer had any means of telling the time.

Never had any human being been as isolated as I was then. After my fainting fall I had cut my head and lost a lot of blood. I could feel that I was covered with it. How sorry I was that I wasn't dead. The ordeal of my final passing still lay ahead of me.

I did not want to think any more. Overwhelmed by pain, I rolled myself up like a ball against the rock and waited for death.

I was just about to lose consciousness again when I heard the faint echo of some sort of distant explosion. It was like a roll of thunder, and I could hear the sound waves gradually fading away in the distant depths of the Earth.

Where was the noise coming from? I imagined that there had been an explosion of gas

My face was wet with tears.

somewhere. I went on listening, in case it came again. Fifteen minutes passed and all I could hear was a terrible silence.

Then a second explosion rang out. At last, I recognized what it was. My uncle and Hans were firing their guns to let me know where they were!

Then I heard another noise. It was voices, and they weren't very far away. I put my ear to the wall and listened. Yes, I could definitely hear someone talking, although I couldn't make out the exact words. They were fuzzy and indistinct.

I wondered if I was hallucinating. But no. Listening closely, I definitely heard the echo of voices. Somebody was talking nearby. I was sure of it.

"Help!" I screamed out. "Help!"

I listened for a reply. There was none. Perhaps my voice had become too weak for them to hear. And it must have been "them" because who else on Earth was down here? The voices must belong to my uncle and Hans.

I stood up and moved slowly along the side of the wall until the sound of the voices became a little clearer. I was getting closer to them. But where were those voices coming from? I thought perhaps that my uncle and Hans were in a parallel tunnel, with a wall between us.

Then I remembered my science lessons at school and how we had done experiments with sound waves. The sound of Uncle and Hans's voices was being transmitted bounce by bounce along the walls of various tunnels.

I decided to try talking at an angle to the wall to see if my voice bounced all the way to them. There was no time to lose. If my companions moved even a few steps away, the sound effect might disappear and I would lose contact with them forever.

"Help!" I screamed out. "Help!"

I drew close to the wall and, speaking as clearly as possible, called out: "Uncle Lidenbrock!"

I waited in extreme anxiety, but at last my call was returned.

"Axel. Is that you?" It was my uncle's voice.

"Yes! Yes!" I replied.

"Where are you, my boy?" he said.

"I'm lost in absolute darkness," I replied.

"But your lamp, Axel?"

"Gone out!" I said.

"And the stream?"

"Disappeared, Uncle."

"We've been searching for you up and down," he said. "And I think we're now as lost as you. But I expect you've noticed this strange sound effect. I can hear you quite clearly. But I have no way of knowing exactly where you are. You might be in a gallery high above me or in a tunnel way below."

"Just keep talking, Uncle," I said, "and I will slowly find my way to you."

"All I can tell you is that we are in a huge cavern with a great many galleries and tunnels leading into it," he said. "The tunnel you are in must eventually lead you to where we are."

As my uncle talked, I started to feel my

"I'm lost in absolute darkness."

way along the wall in the direction of his voice. He kept talking all the time, to guide me. The passage began to slope steeply away from me. I sat down and started to let myself slide.

Soon the speed of my descent increased at an alarming rate. It quickly became not so much a slide, as a fall. I tumbled into space and felt myself falling down a vertical shaft, bouncing off sharp rocky projections. My head hit a rock and once again, I lost consciousness.

Chapter 16
Saved!

When I awoke I was in semi-darkness, stretched out on some thick vegetation. I thought it was a variety of moss. My uncle was kneeling beside me, watching my face for signs of life. At my first sigh, he took my hand. And when I fully opened my eyes, he gave a cry of joy.

"He's awake! He's awake!"

"Yes," I replied feebly.

"My dear boy," he said. "You're saved!"

I was deeply touched by my uncle's words. I had never seen such tenderness in the Professor before.

Next it was Hans's turn to welcome me back from the dead. He just gave me a huge smile.

"Tell me, Uncle, where I am," I said.

"In good time," he replied. "Now just rest and get better. You need sleep."

"At least tell me the day," I said.

"It's eleven o'clock at night and it's Sunday, 9 August," he said.

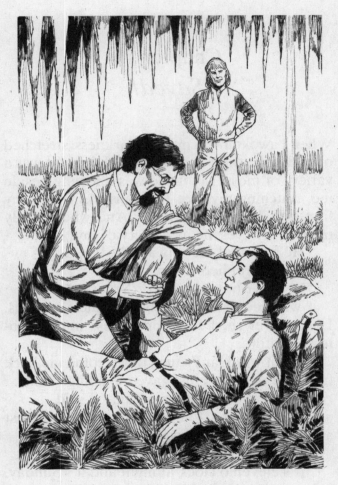

My uncle was kneeling beside me.

Saved!

I was still very weak and my eyes shut of their own accord. I fell into a deep sleep of exhaustion.

The next morning, I awoke and saw my new surroundings more clearly. I was in a delightful grotto adorned with magnificent stalactites, which were hanging from the roof.

There was no lamp or torch burning. Yet, inexplicably, gleams of light were filtering into the grotto. I could also hear a vague, mysterious murmur; something like the sound of waves breaking on a shore. And I also thought I could hear something like the whistling of the wind.

I wondered whether I was awake or dreaming. Perhaps I had cracked my head in the fall so badly that I was hearing things. But I looked at the light again. It really was a ray of daylight. That really was the sound of the waves and the wind.

Had my uncle brought me to the surface again? Had he given up the expedition? Or had he already been to the center of the Earth and returned?

Just then the Professor appeared. "Good morning, Axel." he said cheerfully. "I'm ready to wager you're feeling better."

"I am indeed," I replied, sitting up.

"That isn't surprising," he said. "We took it in turns to watch over you last night and we saw you getting better all the time."

My uncle then prepared some breakfast for me. "It really was a miracle that you weren't killed in the fall down that shaft," he said. "But at least it brought you down to us again. I have no idea how we got separated."

"Are none of my bones broken?" I asked.

"None," he smiled.

"What about my head?"

"Just a few bruises and a nasty cut," was the reply. "Your head is still set most firmly on your shoulders."

"Have we returned to the surface?" I asked.

"No. What makes you think that?"

"Because I can see daylight. I can hear the wind and the sea."

"Oh! Is that all?" he said matter-of-factly, trying not to grin.

"Won't you explain?" I begged him.

"I can't explain it," he said. "I can't explain it because it is inexplicable. But you shall see for yourself, and then you'll realize that geologists still have a lot to learn."

"Then let's go outside," I cried, struggling to my feet. "Show me the inexplicable."

Saved!

"Have we returned to the surface?"

"No, Axel," he said. "The open air might be bad for you."

"The open air?" I said, quite shocked.

"Yes, the wind is rather strong today. I don't want to risk you going out in it."

My uncle sounded like a fussing mother, worried about me catching a cold.

"I tell you Uncle, I feel perfectly well," I insisted.

"Have patience, my boy," he said. "A relapse would cause us a lot of trouble and we have no time to lose, for the voyage may be a long one."

"The voyage?" I mumbled, feeling confused.

"Yes, you rest first and tomorrow we set sail," replied my uncle.

"Set sail!" I gasped, quite astounded.

Did he mean there was a river or a lake outside? Was there a ship at anchor, waiting for us? Was there an underground harbor out there?

My curiosity was roused to fever pitch and there was no way my uncle could hold me back. I got up, wrapped a rug around my shoulders, and went out of the grotto.

Chapter 17
Another World

At first I saw nothing. My eyes, which had become accustomed to darkness, abruptly closed in the glare. When I finally managed to open them again, I was astounded.

"The sea!" I gasped.

"Yes," said my uncle. "We have named it the Lidenbrock Sea. I don't think any scientist will dispute that I discovered it."

A vast sheet of water stretched into the distance. There was a large beach with waves breaking onto it.

I could see everything, but not because of the sun. There was no sun, nor moon or stars, as I discovered later. Yet there was a constant light. The whole scene was lit by dazzling shafts of brilliance. It was a sort of dancing light, constantly on the move. I had no idea where it came from.

There wasn't a real sky, either. Where the sky might have been there was a vast dome of granite. Now and again occasional clouds did cross that bizarre ceiling. They must have been formed by some process involving fiery gases, because they often burst into flames.

Behind the beach was a line of huge cliffs. Never had I seen such tall cliffs before.

The scene had a rather sad, lonely look to it, and I guessed it was because there was no real sun. I must admit the whole place baffled me.

I turned to my uncle. Surely he could explain it all.

"This is geology turned on its head," he said. "I know of no such geological formation that could have created this mini-world, or this sea. Are you strong enough to walk for a while?"

"Yes!" I cried, eager to explore this strange place.

My uncle had already put Hans to work collecting wood, to make a raft. Not content with trying to reach the center of the Earth, he also wanted to explore the sea that he had named after himself.

So we set off. On top of the cliffs was a dense forest, or at least what looked like one. When we got closer, we found there were no actual trees in the forest. It was made up of giant mushrooms thirty feet high. However,

Another World

The whole place baffled me.

there were lots of primitive-looking trees elsewhere.

Beneath the cliffs, all sorts of flowers were growing. The Professor recognized several of them.

"Many of these have been extinct for millions of years . . . in our world, that is," he said, staring at them in amazement. "But I can recognize them from fossil records. Here they still live on, as in a perfect museum, showing what was growing in the world during its earliest days. It's astonishing! Magnificent! Splendid! Awe-inspiring!"

"What about creatures?" I asked. "Have you seen any?"

"Look beneath your feet," he said.

I looked down and saw that the beach was littered with animal bones. "What are they, Uncle?"

"The bones of many long-dead and extinct creatures," he said. "Look—here are the jaw and tail bones of a dinosaur, and the wing bones of a flying lizard."

"How do we know," I asked a little nervously, "that some of these creatures aren't still living here? Perhaps they still roam the mushroom forest."

The bones of many long-dead creatures.

"I'm sure they do," said the Professor. "If we can see some of the world's first plants, then there is no reason why we shouldn't see the earliest animals in this strange place."

While the Professor returned to the grotto to see how Hans was getting on, I stayed outside for a while. I found my way to a rocky promontory and sat there, looking around and wondering at all I saw.

Where did the sea end? Why was it there? Was it linked somehow to our own oceans in the upper world?

I saw a little cove in the distance, and imagined a great sailing ship setting out on this wonderful sea. Of course, there was no ship.

As I thought about all these things, the wind finally dropped altogether. A calm and peaceful silence came over this baffling world we had discovered.

Chapter 18
Voyage on the Lidenbrock Sea

I slept well that night, and the following day I awoke feeling better than ever. I raced down to the sea for a swim. It was delightfully warm and refreshing.

At breakfast my uncle mentioned the tide. "It's rising now and we mustn't miss the chance to study this phenomenon," he said.

"The tide!" I exclaimed.

"Yes, of course," said my uncle.

"You mean that the influence of Earth's moon can be felt all the way down here?" I said. "Can it really push and pull the tides through granite, and all the other rocks we have passed through?"

"Why not?" he answered. "I'm sure you will see it rise and fall, just like the Atlantic Ocean."

Once we stood on the beach again, I could see that he spoke the truth. The tide was rising.

"You know, Uncle," I said, "I can scarcely believe my eyes. Who on Earth would ever imagine that inside our planet is a real sea, with real tides and winds. It's unbelievable."

"Why shouldn't there be?" the Professor said. "There's no law of science against it. And who knows, there may be other subterranean oceans."

"And what fish can we expect in these waters?" I wanted to know.

"There are fishing lines and hooks in our stores," he said. "We'll find out later."

"Where exactly are we now, Uncle?" I asked.

"We're nearly nine hundred horizontal miles from Iceland and eighty-eight miles deep. The Scottish Highlands are immediately above us now. All the highest mountains in Scotland are now bearing down on us."

I asked my uncle whether he was considering turning back now and returning to the surface. "Of course not, my boy," he said. "We shall continue our journey, seeing that everything has gone well so far."

"But what about the sea?" I asked. "How can we get below this ocean?"

"Oh we won't go through it," he replied, pointing over to Hans. "It's probably surrounded by a mass of granite. We will take to the water on our raft and search for a way down."

He took me to see where Hans had cut down what he called "fossil trees". They had died long ago but were still buoyant enough to float.

By the following day, Hans had finished his task. The raft was about ten feet long and five feet wide. It was a very solid craft with the timbers jointed together for extra strength. It had a mast and sail, and a tiller to steer with.

Hans officially named the craft after me. So it was he who launched the *Axel* onto my uncle's *Lidenbrock Sea.*

The next day, Friday, 13 August, we got aboard with all our provisions and equipment, and raised our sail. Just as we were leaving, my uncle stood up and pointed to where we had stayed for the last few days.

"We must name this place," he said. "Let's call it *Port Grauben*, after your fiancée."

"Port Grauben it will be," I said proudly.

There was a good wind that day and we raced away.

"At this rate," said my uncle, "we'll cover at least seventy-five miles in twenty-four hours."

That evening, Hans put out a fishing line

"We will take to the water on our raft."

and caught a strange fish. It had no eyes and no fins.

"What is it, Uncle?" I asked excitedly.

"It belongs to a family of fish that has long been extinct in our waters," he said. "I've seen a fossil of this fish, in the Hamburg museum. How my colleagues there would envy me seeing a live version of their fossil!"

By Saturday we were far out to sea with no coastline visible. The Professor kept searching the horizon with his telescope, but saw nothing.

"I wonder if Arne Saknussemm came this way," I said. "Did he have to cross this sea, do you think?"

"I have a feeling he might have," said my uncle.

The next day we were still out of sight of land. It was a bigger ocean than we ever imagined.

Uncle couldn't tell how large his ocean was, so he decided to find out how deep it was. He tied a heavy axe to a long rope and dropped it over the side, feeding out the rope yard by yard. We didn't find the bottom. The rope ran out.

When we raised the axe we found some strange marks on the iron head.

Hans caught a strange fish.

"Teeth marks!" said my uncle. "And it would have to be a mighty powerful pair of jaws to make those marks on the head of an iron axe."

We now knew we were not alone at sea. Those teeth marks could have been made by some gigantic prehistoric specimen. What sort of monster was lurking below? A giant shark? A prehistoric whale? A marine murderer from millions of years back in time?

My mind was quickly filling up with nightmarish visions.

Chapter 19
Battle of the Monsters

The sight of those teeth marks made me try to remember what I had been taught about prehistory. Earlier, the Professor and I had been talking about what geological period we thought the ocean belonged to.

We had agreed that the sea probably fitted in somewhere between the Jurassic and Cretaceous periods. That was because the cliffs we had seen were primarily made of chalk, a feature of those times. They were also times when dinosaurs ruled the land, and other huge monsters such as ichthyosaurs and plesiosaurs held sway in the oceans.

No human eye had ever seen such monsters alive. They had all lived many thousands of years before man had evolved. I had seen some skeletons of ichthyosaurs in museums. But the thought of them alive and possibly swimming beneath me, started me shaking.

I gazed in terror at the sea, dreading to see

one of the prehistoric creatures emerge from the depths. I think my uncle was thinking the same thing. After seeing the marks on the axe, he hadn't stopped staring anxiously at the waves.

"Why the devil did my uncle have to find out the depth of the water?" I thought. "All he's done is stir up some evil creature in its lair."

I checked that our guns were all in good order. My uncle saw me and nodded his approval.

Then I saw something. The surface of the water had begun to move and shiver over a wide area. Something large was moving just below the surface. We held our breath, and

Something large was just below the surface.

121

then the sea calmed down again. Whatever had been lurking beneath us had moved away. But we knew that from now on we had to keep a good lookout.

***

With no sun to sink and no moon to rise, there was no night on the Lidenbrock Sea. A world without a sun or a moon was a most unromantic place. But it did mean that we could always see what was happening on the surface of the sea, although I for one would rather have been able to see what lurked beneath it.

One evening I was dozing at the back of the raft when a violent shock woke me. The raft had been lifted right out of the water with indescribable force and hurled a hundred feet or more. It crashed back to the sea again, almost capsizing.

"What on earth . . ." I cried out.

"What on earth indeed," said my uncle, pointing to a dark mass speeding away from us.

"It was a colossal porpoise," he said. "It's got the head and neck of a dinosaur and the teeth of a crocodile. It's the long-extinct plesiosaur. I'm sure of it."

"It was a colossal porpoise."

Just then I saw another gigantic dolphin-like creature, not far off. Its huge teeth were set in a long, pointed nose. "What's that, Uncle?" I asked.

"Oh my goodness," he gasped. "This is all too much. Just to see this creature alive is beyond belief. It's an ichthyosaur!"

All around us now were other members of the same two marine families. It looked as though war had been declared between the two species.

The three of us just stood and stared in wonder at this gathering of monsters, so long extinct in our world. They were all of supernatural size and strength. The smallest of them could have eaten our raft as if it were the tiniest morsel.

I must admit I had seen enough of these monsters, and wished I was back in the grotto. But there was no return now. As we looked back, we saw that our way was blocked by other monsters coming to join the battle. Escape was out of the question.

The creatures were very close to us now and traveling at great speed. I picked up my rifle, but I quickly realized a bullet would hardly tickle one of these giants.

They attacked with terrifying fury.

Then, as if someone had fired a starting gun, the plesiosaurs and ichthyosaurs charged at each other. They attacked with terrifying fury, raising mountainous waves that threatened to capsize us.

One by one the creatures were either killed or driven off, until only one of each species was left. They were true giants. The plesiosaur was more than fifty feet long, its huge neck swaying above the surface of the sea. Most of the ichthyosaur was hidden beneath the waves, but we all heard the snapping of its teeth as it furiously thrashed about in the water.

These two animals set about each other with only one object—to kill the other. And the fight wasn't a quick one. After two hours they were still battling, locked together for long periods.

Suddenly the pair disappeared beneath the surface, creating a huge whirlpool where they had been. Several minutes passed. Was the fight going to end in the depths of the sea? All at once, an enormous head shot out of the water. It had once belonged to the plesiosaur. The ichthyosaur had bitten its enemy's head off.

The victor swam off, leaving us in peace.

Chapter 20
The Geyser

The next day we heard a loud roar, far in the distance. Hans climbed to the top of the mast to look ahead. He saw nothing but the sea stretching away toward the empty horizon.

Hour by hour, the roar became louder and louder. I was sure it was a distant waterfall, although my uncle shook his head. Soon the roar became so loud we could hardly hear ourselves speak. If I was right about the waterfall, then it must be one big enough to carry a whole ocean over it.

Late in the afternoon, Hans climbed the mast again. Now he saw something and pointed to the horizon. We looked out and saw nothing at first. Then I spotted what I thought was a grey cloud approaching.

"It's a huge jet of water," said my uncle.

"Another sea monster," I replied. "Shouldn't we steer a course away from it?"

"It's a huge jet of water."

"Never," said the Professor. "We are explorers. We must head straight for it."

I estimated the animal must be about thirty miles from us. If it was a creature, it had to be of superhuman proportions because the jet grew bigger and bigger, the closer we got to it. What kind of a monster could it be?

As we came within about five miles of the beast, we began to see its shape. Its dark, hillocky body lay in the sea like an island. I thought it must be a mile long. It was motionless and apparently asleep. The sea was lapping at its sides. The jet of water, now rising to well over five hundred feet, was falling like a great rain storm.

I thought the creature might be a giant whale. Terror seized me. I refused to go any closer. "We must sail away," I cried, swearing I would pull down the mast unless we did as I said.

"Don't worry," said my uncle. "It's quite clear to me that it's not a creature but an island, and that jet is a hot water geyser pumping from some huge underground lake."

The Professor was right. As we drew nearer, the dimensions of the geyser were revealed to be truly amazing. The jet was touching the clouds. My uncle named the island and its geyser after me.

That evening I took some special observations with the Professor's equipment, to check where my island was. We had sailed 675 miles from Port Grauben. We had also journeyed 1,550 miles in total. My island was beneath England!

The next day the wind dropped away to nothing and the atmosphere grew heavy. There was a strange silence over the ocean. It was as if nature was holding its breath. Our raft lay motionless on a sluggish, flat sea.

Suddenly, I saw the Professor's hair stand on end. I felt mine do the same, and Hans's long red hair followed soon after. The air had become full of electricity. A huge storm was coming!

The southern horizon turned black as terrifying dark clouds bubbled up and began to race towards us. Soon they darkened the whole sky and hid everything from sight. Then from that same horizon came a dreadful howling sound . . .

A moment later, we were hit by a hurricane of unearthly power. It churned up the sea and sent huge waves racing across its surface.

A huge storm was coming!

The raft rose in the air and bounded forward, flinging my uncle head over heels. I crawled over to him and found him clinging to a cable, apparently enjoying the sight of such a violent storm.

"Isn't it wonderful?" he roared against the wind.

Now the raft was truly racing. I called for Hans to lower the sail. But the Professor refused to let him. "We must go where the wind takes us!" he cried.

It was now impossible to work out where we were heading. Were we racing towards the southern horizon? Or was it racing toward us? Who could tell? Thunder and lightning joined the storm. Zigzagging lightning lit our path, rebounding off the granite vault above our heads.

We hung on grimly, expecting to be hit by lightning or sucked into the ocean at any moment.

Chapter 21

An Ancient Graveyard

I prayed for the storm to end, but it just seemed to get worse. It howled and roared for two more days. We could not eat or drink. We could not speak, for the power of the wind sucked our breath away.

If we had thought that nothing worse could happen, we were wrong. We were hit by a fireball that appeared from nowhere. It circled above us for several minutes, before bursting eerily into a hundred small bolts of lightning.

Still the raft raced on, guided by some unseen hand. We were moving at an incalcul-able speed. We must have passed under England, under the English Channel, under France, and perhaps under the whole of Europe.

Then, above the horrendous noise of the storm, I heard an even louder roar. It sounded as if the wild sea had run into a mountain, and we were about to be dashed against it!

The fireball circled above us for several minutes.

That was the last thing I remembered, until I recovered consciousness and found myself lying on a beach. The Professor and Hans were sitting beside me, and the overturned raft was close by. It seemed that we had been thrown ashore.

The storm was over and the raging sea was calming, even as I watched. The Professor was in very good spirits. He had some amusing news for me, too.

"As you can see, we've reached land, dear boy," he said. "My latest calculations put us beneath Germany. And better still, right beneath Hamburg."

The city of Hamburg was our home! I could imagine the Professor's house right above me, and I could see my dear Grauben making breakfast. It seemed strange to be so close, yet so far from home. Physically we were just a hundred miles beneath the city, but a world away in reality.

I felt quite homesick, but nothing could dampen my uncle's happy mood.

"At last!" he cried. "We have reached land again. Now we can really get going and plunge even farther into the depths of the Earth."

"But what about getting back?" I asked.

"When will we start to go home?"

"My boy," he sighed, shaking his head, "how can you think of going back when we haven't even reached our destination?"

"At least tell me how you think we'll find our way back at the end of the journey," I said.

"By the simplest way possible," he replied. "Once we have reached the center of the planet, we shall either find some new route to the surface or go back the way we came."

"But have we enough food?" I asked.

Nothing could dampen my uncle's happy mood.

"We still have plenty of food," he said. "And Hans can always catch us some more fish."

"Did we lose anything in the storm?" I asked.

"Yes," he said. "The guns were washed overboard, although we still have some dry dynamite and gunpowder. All my instruments are safe, too. So at least we'll still know when we reach the center. Otherwise we might travel on and come up on the other side of the world, in Australia!"

The next day we set about exploring the new landscape. We quickly came upon an extraordinary sight. It was an area of rocks that had clearly been hit by some eruption from below. The rocks were solid, but had been through a molten stage.

We were advancing over these rocks when we found what I can only describe as an ancient graveyard. It looked like a huge cemetery, covered with great mounds of bones. Both the Professor and I could recognize many of them.

I was stupefied. Even my uncle was shocked. Here before us, in the form of bones, lay the entire history of early animal life. We were faced with a collection of animal skeletons that

Exploring the new landscape.

any museum would have paid a fortune for; the whole dinosaur family tree alone was represented, with dozens of its ancient ancestors.

But, strange to tell, we were to see something even more spectacular in that graveyard. It was my uncle who found it.

Hans and I heard a shocked cry from him. He had just picked up something.

"Look, Axel," he said in a quavering voice. "Look at this!"

In his hands was a giant human skull.

Chapter 22
Prehistoric Man

"What!" I cried. "A human head?"

"A human head, indeed," said my uncle. "And I suspect it won't be the only one we find here."

He was right; within a few minutes he had found many more human bones. He had also discovered several fully fossilized human beings, complete with rocky hair, teeth, and skin. The most extraordinary thing about them was their size. In life, they must have been twelve feet high.

They made an astonishing sight. I wondered about where they had come from. Had they been living on Earth in prehistoric times? Had their skeletons simply slipped through some geological fault line and ended up here?

Or had they been born into this subterranean world, living and dying like the inhabitants of the upper world?

So far, we had seen only two kinds of living

The bones were an astonishing sight.

creatures here; sea monsters and fish. Was it possible that some human beings, native to this strange land, could still be roaming these desolate shores?

We spent an hour walking among all the bones, before going inland to explore a forest area. And there we had another shock.

We were quietly walking along when we came on a herd of mastodons . . . not fossilized creatures, but living mammals!

I warned my uncle about going any farther. "We haven't got guns any more," I said. "It's too dangerous."

"Well," said the Professor. "It doesn't seem dangerous to one particular man."

"What do you mean?" I said.

"Look over there at the back of the herd," he said, pointing with his arm.

I looked back and gasped. There, not a hundred yards away, was a man!

I could hardly believe what I was seeing. But it was true. Not only was he a man, but he was close to twelve feet tall.

This mastodon shepherd, as I thought he must be, was almost as big as the members of his flock. His head was the size of a buffalo's and in his hand was a giant shepherd's crook.

The Professor was all for trying to communicate with the shepherd, but just then the animals saw us and started to charge. So we retreated along the path we had come.

On the way back we found another extraordinary object. It was a rusty dagger with a twisted blade. It was lying on top of a rock, as if someone had just left it there the day before.

My uncle examined it. "It's quite old," he said. "A few hundred years, perhaps. The point of the blade has been worn away, but the air down here has preserved it well."

He continued looking at it and then wandered around the rock on which it had been found. Then, with growing excitement, he went on. "The riddle is solved," he announced. "This dagger must be sixteenth century. Axel, we have made a great discovery. This blade has lain here for three hundred years."

"But it didn't get here by itself," I said.

"No indeed," he said. "Someone has been here before us."

"What! Someone else?"

"Yes," he said, "and if I'm not mistaken, that person has left something else for us to find."

The Professor knelt down beside the rock

The animals started to charge.

and examined it very closely. "Aha!" he cried. "I have it! Look! Look, Axel!"

I knelt down and examined the spot that his finger was pointing at. I saw that two initials had been carved in the rock. And beside them was a pointing arrow.

"This can only mean one thing," said my uncle, his voice full of excitement. "We have made a find of the utmost importance, my boy!"

Chapter 23
Saknussemm's Arrow

I guessed what my uncle was about to announce before he said it.

"The letters on the rock are A and S," he said. "Arne Saknussemm, the Icelandic explorer. So he did find his way to the center of the Earth. And this is our proof. He's showing us the way! He carved his initials into the rock with that knife. That's why it's blunt and slightly twisted."

Since the beginning of our journey, I'd had so many surprises that I might be forgiven for thinking that nothing else could astound me. Yet at the sight of those two letters, carved there three hundred years earlier, I stood in utter astonishment. Not only were the initials clear, but I was now holding the very knife that had made them.

For the first time, I truly believed in the existence of Saknussemm and the reality of his journey all those years ago. The arrow was pointing to a wooded hill about half a mile away. The three of us ran all the way. We entered the wood and began searching.

After several hours of hunting, we were exhausted. We had found no clue to what Arne Saknussemm had hoped to reveal to us. We decided we were wasting our time. Whatever had been here in Saknussemm's time must have disappeared.

We were walking out of the wood when Hans, who was following us, cried out. My uncle and I turned and saw that he had fallen into some kind of dip in the ground.

We hurried back and hauled him out. That action resulted in a sudden collapse of earth and rocks around the dip. Now we saw that it hid the entrance to a tunnel.

We peered inside the tunnel. Dark and musty, it led sharply downward.

"The man's a genius," said the Professor. "He obviously left behind the arrow to show future travelers the way and I have no doubt that when we reach the center of the Earth, we will find his mark again."

I have to admit at this stage that I was now as enthusiastic as my uncle in hoping to reach the heart of our planet. I had forgotten about

Hauling Hans out of the dip.

the dangers ahead, and also the perils of the return. Saknussemm had been and returned. What he had done, I could do too.

"Forward! Forward! Forward to the center of the Earth!" I cried.

But even my uncle wasn't quite ready to leave yet. He wanted to make a base camp there, where we could store all the things we didn't need to take. He asked Hans to get the raft and leave it by the tunnel entrance. "We might need it again," he said.

That evening, with everything ready, we prepared to leave. "It's good to see you so excited and enthusiastic again," the Professor said to me. "You're even more excited than I am."

So we set off again. The new tunnel was about five feet wide and it was worn smooth by the molten lava that had once flooded up from below. We made good progress, but suddenly we found the tunnel completely blocked by a huge rock. There was no way around it. It must have fallen since Saknussemm's day.

Luckily, Hans had the answer. He hurried back to our base camp and returned with the dynamite and gunpowder. He laid a huge charge and attached a very long fuse.

"This is going to be some explosion," said my uncle. "I think it best if we light the fuse and head out to sea in the raft to be absolutely sure we don't get hit by falling debris."

So that's what we did. Hans lit the fuse and joined us on the raft. We hurriedly rowed ourselves out to a safe distance.

The explosion, when it came, was enormous. The fact that the charge had been laid in a small tunnel trebled its power. As we watched, the whole hill above the tunnel exploded. Huge rocks flew into the sky, some narrowly missing our raft.

Suddenly, the whole landscape had changed. The hill had vanished and a bottomless pit had appeared where the original tunnel entrance had been.

Our raft started to twist, as if it was caught in some strange current. The boat was spinning around quite fast now. I had the distinct impression that we were being sucked down, rather like bath water is pulled down the drainpipe.

That was exactly what was happening. The bottomless pit created by the explosion was sucking in the sea, creating a torrent. And we

The explosion was enormous.

were being dragged in too.

There was no escaping now. Soon we would all be drowned!

Chapter 24
A Nightmare Ride

None of us remembered exactly what happened immediately after the explosion. We clung to the raft as we were thrown violently into the huge watery chasm. The raft was completely out of control, and being pulled downward at speed by the torrent.

It was like a violent fairground ride. We rolled this way and that, often hitting unseen rocks. Soon we were sucked into a new tunnel and sent flying down what must have been a near vertical drop. Somehow we managed to hold onto the raft, and each other.

Judging by the air whipping past my face, we must have been traveling faster than the fastest express locomotive. Occasionally, the raft was caught by an eddy and spun around. But for the most part, the rushing water held us in a firm grip.

After a while, we managed to feel a little less out of control. Hans even managed to get one

It was like a violent fairground ride.

of our remaining electric lamps going. At that moment we shot out of the tunnel and into a vast gallery. The torrent of water didn't slow down at all. If anything, it was speeding up. I estimated that we were traveling at about ninety miles an hour.

I also saw that all our food had been swept overboard. I looked across at my uncle and saw that he was still grimly holding onto his essential instruments. I started to laugh hysterically. Why was I worried about losing our food when this flood was taking us straight to our graves?

At that moment the electric lamp sputtered, and suddenly gave out. Water had seeped inside it. We were plunged into total darkness.

Still the raft sped on. We were going faster than ever. I closed my eyes, waiting for the end and hoping it would come quickly and painlessly. The descent was definitely becoming steeper. Gravity was trying to remove us from the raft.

The ride couldn't go on much longer. We all were losing strength and soon, we would not be able to hold onto the raft. Worse still, the raft was now being banged so hard into the rocks around us that we were knocked almost senseless. It was as if the gods of the underworld

We were knocked almost senseless.

didn't want us to see their secrets, so they had decided to destroy us.

Down, down, down we raced, until I began to detect that we were finally slowing. A few minutes later, the raft slowed down enough for Hans to finally light our last electric lamp.

We only had a second to glance at our surroundings before a new swell of water took hold of us and swept us upward again.

"What happening, Uncle?" I called out.

"The water has reached the bottom of the abyss," he replied, "and is now rising until it finds its own level. I think we are in a narrow shaft. It'll be a miracle if we get out of it alive."

We both realized that the temperature was also rising quickly. It must have been forty degrees centigrade by then.

"If we aren't crushed to death or drowned," I said, "we might even be burnt to death."

My uncle shrugged his shoulders. "While the heart still beats, there is always some hope," he said.

"What hope?" I wondered. "What chance of escaping with our lives now?"

Chapter 25
Inferno!

The temperature was rising fast. I felt as though I was burning up.

"Are we going toward a furnace?" I asked, briefly touching the wall as we continued on up. It was red hot.

I also got splashed with water, and it was boiling. A hopeless terror took hold of me and I felt that a catastrophe was approaching. I had no definite idea about what was going to happen, but I knew something was going on. Something I didn't understand.

The rocks surrounding us had started to heave and creak. Steam was billowing from the walls. I managed to glance at my uncle's compass. It had gone mad. The needle was swinging jerkily from north to south and west to east. Then it began to giddily spin in circles.

Now I could hear explosions far below us. It was as if we were inside a thunder cloud. The compass spun even more wildly. Was the

Inferno!

A catastrophe was approaching.

Earth's crust about to burst? Were we about to be sucked into molten rock, only to be reborn as fossils in millions of years' time?

I looked at my uncle. He seemed calmly resigned to whatever fate befell him now.

"What's happening, Uncle?" I shouted again. "The walls are shaking. The rock's quivering. The awful heat. The spinning compass. It must be an earthquake."

"I think you're mistaken, my boy," he replied.

"But all the signs tell me it is an earthquake," I said.

"No," he insisted. "I'm expecting something a little more dramatic than an earthquake."

"More dramatic!" I exclaimed. "Nothing can be more dramatic than this!"

"How about an eruption, Axel?" he said, with a deadpan expression on his face.

"An eruption?" I gasped. "You mean, you think we are in the shaft of an active volcano?"

"I do," nodded the Professor. "And I think it's the best thing that could happen to us."

The best thing? I wondered if my uncle had gone out of his mind. What did he mean? And how could he be so calm?

Inferno!

"What!" I cried. "We are caught in the middle of an eruption. Fate has flung us into a path of burning lava, molten rock, and boiling water. We are going to be thrown out, expelled, rejected, vomited, spat out into the air in a whirlwind of flame, red hot lava, fragments of rock, and a storm of ashes and cinders. And you say it's the best thing that could happen to us?"

"Yes," replied my uncle, "because it's our only chance of returning to the Earth's surface."

"Nothing can be more dramatic than this!"

I supposed he was right. But I'm sure that even he realized we had no hope of surviving such an extreme journey.

The noise around us was getting louder and louder. I was suffocating in the heat.

I wondered why we were still alive. How on earth had our raft held together? It should have exploded into flames by now. I suddenly realized that the answer lay in the fossilized wood Hans had used to make it. It was unburnable.

The raft seemed quite at home in this inferno as the boiling water forced us up this volcanic path. Yet we all knew our luck wouldn't hold out much longer. As death neared, I wondered where we would emerge. In what part of the world would we be shot out into the air? Where would our bodies be found?

I felt our raft suddenly increase speed yet again. The water which had carried us had all but evaporated into steam. We were now rising under the power of combustible forces never experienced by man before. Then suddenly, we stopped. All was silent, except a few groans from far below us.

"I wonder what is happening now," I said weakly.

"This is very normal," said the Professor, as if he was lecturing a class. "Eruptions are not always instant. Sometimes they stop and start again, building up their power."

"Does that mean we won't be thrown out of the volcano?" I asked.

"Oh no," he said. "We'll be thrown out, for sure. But the volcano will do it in its own time. From my calculations this one seems to erupt every ten minutes. So we should be on our way again quite soon."

He was right. A short time later we were shot upward again at a tremendous speed. How we held onto the raft and each other, I will never know.

This happened several more times as we drew ever closer to the Earth's surface.

The Professor tried to cheer us up by suggesting that perhaps we were not in the main shaft. He said that we might be in a side vent, and that might help us to survive.

During those short minutes when the eruption halted, we were almost overcome with the heat and fumes. And each time we set off again, it was with even more force and fury than before.

I have no clear recollection what happened

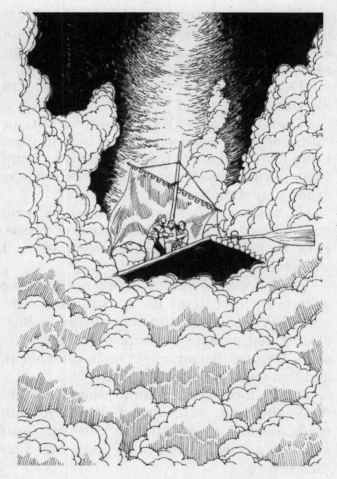

We shot upward at a tremendous speed.

during the last part of our incredible journey up through the volcano. I vaguely remember a wall of flame flying past us and seeing my uncle's face for what I thought would be the last time.

The feeling I had was that of a man trapped inside the barrel of a cannon . . . a man about to be fired into the air.

That was my last thought before blacking out once more.

Chapter 26
The Island of Stromboli

When I opened my eyes again, I found Hans holding me by my belt with one hand and my unconscious uncle with the other. I was not seriously injured, but bruised all over. We were lying on a steep mountain slope, only a few feet from the edge of a cliff. If Hans hadn't hung onto us, my uncle and I would undoubtedly have tumbled to our deaths.

"Where are we?" asked my uncle, when he came to.

"I think we are back on our Earth," I said, hopefully.

The Professor seemed to be extremely annoyed at returning to the surface of his planet. His mission had been rudely interrupted by the volcanic eruption.

"And exactly what part of the Earth are we on?" he asked.

Hans and I shrugged our shoulders.

After the countless surprises of our journey,

We were lying on a steep mountain slope.

one more had been reserved for us. I had expected to see a volcano covered with perpetual snow beneath Icelandic skies.

But no. I was laying halfway down a mountain baked by a scorching sun. I could not believe it. After experiencing so much dark, the sun almost blinded me.

"We're certainly not in Iceland," said the Professor.

We looked about. Five hundred feet above us was the volcano which had clearly just ejected us. It was still breathing fire and brimstone. A little way off we could see where the main channel of molten lava was flowing down the slopes.

The Professor had been right. We must have been thrown out of a side vent. If we had been ejected from the main vent we would have been turned into red hot lava and sent sliding down the mountainside as molten human beings.

We started to get our bearings. We were on an island. Far below us to the south was a small harbor, with boats bobbing up and down on an exquisitely beautiful tropical sea.

"Our volcano is still erupting," said my uncle. "It would be a pity to survive being thrown out of it, only to be hit on the head by a piece of rock. Let's go down, and then we'll find out where are. Besides, I'm dying of thirst."

So we set off, slipping and sliding down the slope, trying to avoid the hot streams of lava flowing down the mountain beside us. It took us all day to get off the mountain. By evening we had reached an orchard. What a joy it was to taste that fruit!

Molten lava was flowing down the slopes.

While we were enjoying the fruit, a child appeared. My uncle questioned the boy, asking him in any number of languages where we were. The boy stood staring vacantly as my uncle tried English, German, French, and Spanish. Finally, in answer to the question in Italian, the boy spoke.

"Stromboli," he said.

We were all astonished. We were on the island of Stromboli, about sixty miles off the western coast of Italy.

Oh what a journey we had been on! What a wonderful journey. What a terrifying journey. We had gone down one volcano and, if this was Stromboli, then we had emerged—still alive—almost three thousand miles away from our departure point.

Chapter 27
Heroes All

We took a boat from the island and reached Messina in Italy. Another boat took us home to Hamburg, in Germany.

I cannot describe my joy at seeing Grauben and Martha. I truly never expected to set eyes on them again.

"My dearest Axel, you are a true hero!" said Grauben. "I always wanted to marry a hero. And now I shall."

The return of Professor Lidenbrock and news of his discoveries caused a sensation in Hamburg, and all around the world. He became a national hero overnight.

A great banquet was organized to celebrate the journey, and after dinner the Professor told the complete story of our travels. He expressed regret that he hadn't actually followed in the exact steps of Arne Saknussemm.

"I would have liked to reach the exact center of the Earth, as Saknussemm must have

The professor became a national hero.

done," he said. "But the adventures we had made up for that."

***

Hans stayed with us for a while, but soon grew homesick and traveled back to Iceland where he too became a hero. He was already a hero in our eyes. We would certainly never have returned alive but for his bravery and silent care.

Of course, there were some people who doubted our story. But among the bits and pieces that the Professor brought back were some bones from the graveyard beside the ocean. One of them, after being examined in a laboratory, turned out to be the earliest known human bone ever found.

Not that the Professor cared if he was or wasn't believed. He knew where he had been and he knew what he had found there. The future was more important to him. He was already planning another journey. This time he was determined to reach the center of the Earth!

I shuddered at the thought of descending to the depths of the Earth again. But then I wondered … The thought of being turned into a premature fossil was a small risk to take, to see amazing prehistoric creatures and witness man's extinct ancestors, still alive, far beneath the surface of the Earth.